The Dragon Takes a Wife

for Pat White
— F.F.

ISBN 0-590-46694-1

Text copyright © 1972 by Walter Dean Myers.
Illustrations copyright © 1995 by Fiona French.
All rights reserved.
Published by Scholastic Inc.
SCHOLASTIC and associated logos are trademarks and/or
registered trademarks of Scholastic Inc.

12 11 10 9 8 7 6 5 4 3 2 1   0 1 2 3 4 5/0

Printed in the U.S.A.   08

First Scholastic Trade paperback printing, September 2000

The illustrator used watercolor, crayon, and gouache
for the paintings in this book.

Text design by Adrienne M. Syphrett
Cover design by Kristina Iulo

The Dragon Takes a Wife

BY
WALTER DEAN MYERS

ILLUSTRATED BY
FIONA FRENCH

SCHOLASTIC INC.
New York Toronto London Auckland Sydney
Mexico City New Delhi Hong Kong

ONCE UPON A TIME, in the ancient kingdom of Lyraland, there lived a good but lonely dragon named Harry.

Harry wanted a wife. But in Lyraland the only way for Harry to get a wife was to prove his courage by winning a battle with the knight in shining armor. And Harry was not a good fighter.

Each week Harry would go to a clearing in the woods to fight the knight, and each week he would lose. Then he would go home and play sad songs on his flute.

Harry knew he needed help. So one day he went over to the other side of the kingdom, where all the good fairies lived.

"What's bugging you, baby?" asked Mabel Mae Jones, one of the sweetest and kindest fairies in the kingdom.

"Well," said Harry, a tear welling in his great dragon's eye, "each week, to prove my courage, I fight the knight in shining armor. And each week I lose. I get lonelier and lonelier. I'd like to win once, so I can get married and live happily ever after."

"I can dig where you're coming from," said Mabel Mae. "What do you think would help you?"

"Perhaps if you made my flame twice as hot as it is now," answered Harry, "I could win."

"That ain't no big thing," said Mabel Mae. "Dig on these magic words I'm going to say. When you go into battle, repeat them to yourself and the magic will work."

Mabel Mae waved her wand and said the magic words.

"Fire, grow red,
Fire, grow bright!
Turn Harry on
So he can burn that knight!"

Harry thanked Mabel Mae and went home. When the time came to fight the knight, he again went to the clearing in the woods. This time, when the knight came charging at him, Harry repeated the magic words to himself and breathed out as hard as he could.

But instead of hot breath, polka dots came floating out of his mouth and up into the sky like balloons. The knight struck Harry on the tail and rode back into the woods.

"Owww!" cried Harry. He went home, put a Band-Aid on his tail, and played another sad song on his flute.

The next morning Harry went back to see Mabel Mae and told her what had happened.

"Well, chill out, honey; ain't nobody perfect," she said. "Let's just try something new."

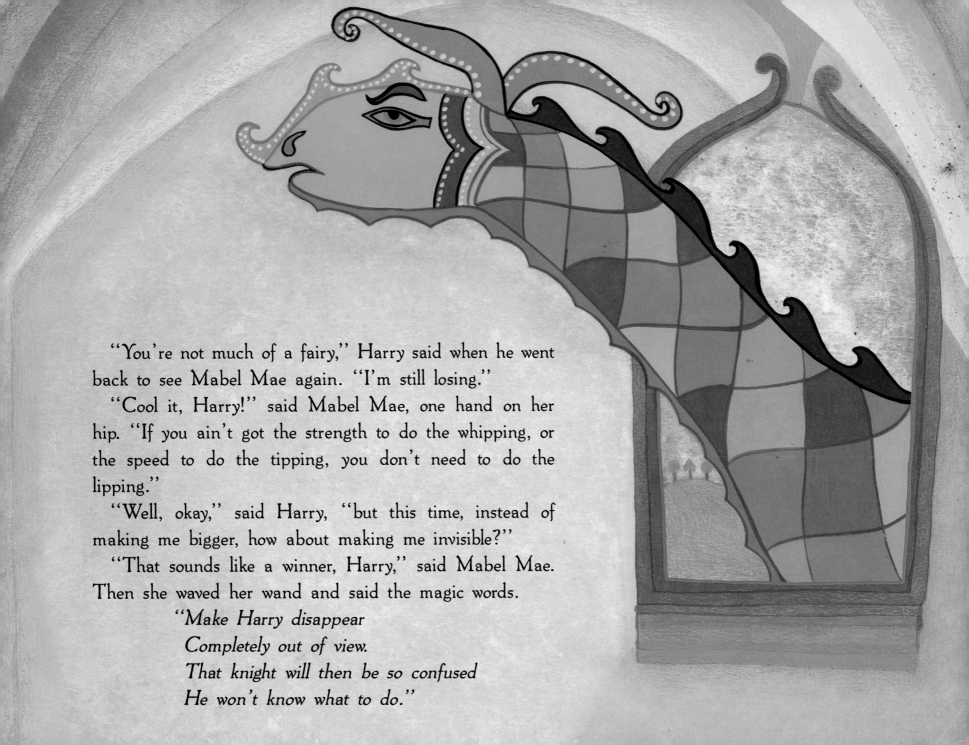

"You're not much of a fairy," Harry said when he went back to see Mabel Mae again. "I'm still losing."

"Cool it, Harry!" said Mabel Mae, one hand on her hip. "If you ain't got the strength to do the whipping, or the speed to do the tipping, you don't need to do the lipping."

"Well, okay," said Harry, "but this time, instead of making me bigger, how about making me invisible?"

"That sounds like a winner, Harry," said Mabel Mae. Then she waved her wand and said the magic words.

> *"Make Harry disappear*
> *Completely out of view.*
> *That knight will then be so confused*
> *He won't know what to do."*

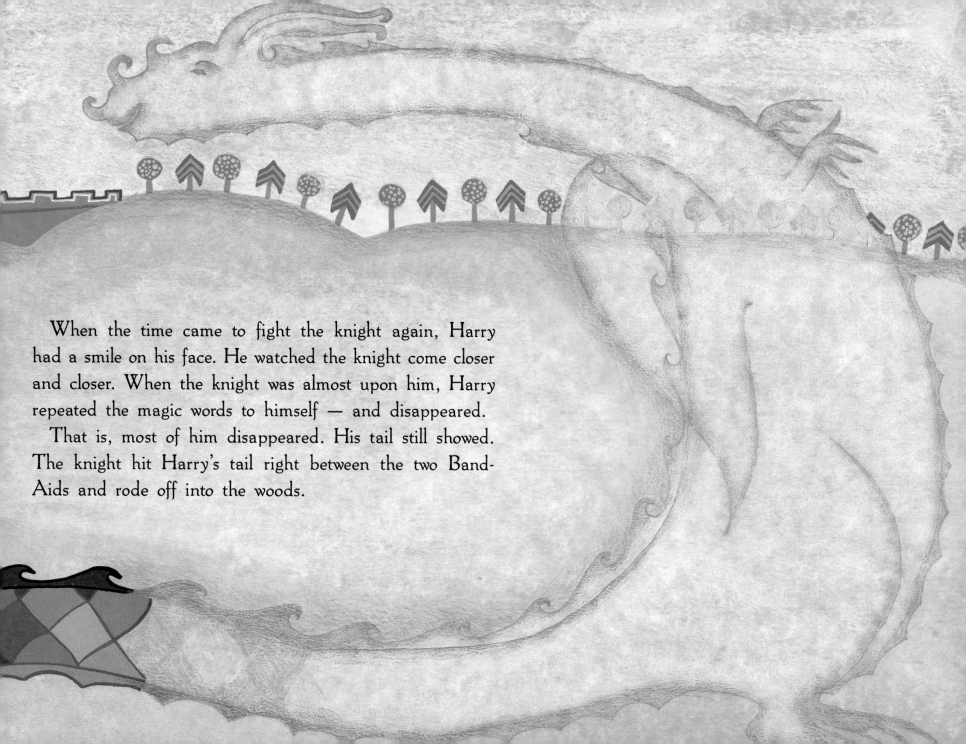

When the time came to fight the knight again, Harry had a smile on his face. He watched the knight come closer and closer. When the knight was almost upon him, Harry repeated the magic words to himself — and disappeared.

That is, most of him disappeared. His tail still showed. The knight hit Harry's tail right between the two Band-Aids and rode off into the woods.

Harry went back to see Mabel Mae again.

"I know, I know," said Mabel Mae, "you got blown away again. Let's face it, baby, that knight can definitely take care of business." Mabel Mae covered her mouth and giggled. "But you did look funny with just your tail showing like that."

"Oh, I'll never win," moaned Harry.

"Do you have any more ideas?"

Harry thought for a moment. "How about a disguise so I can trick the knight?" he said.

"Sounds good to me," Mabel Mae said. "When the knight charges, you turn into the border of the page and you'll have him surrounded!"

"That sounds good!" Harry beamed.

Mabel Mae waved her wand and said the magic words.

> *"Fairy power, dragon power,*
> *We're both in a rage;*
> *Make old Harry*
> *The border of the page."*

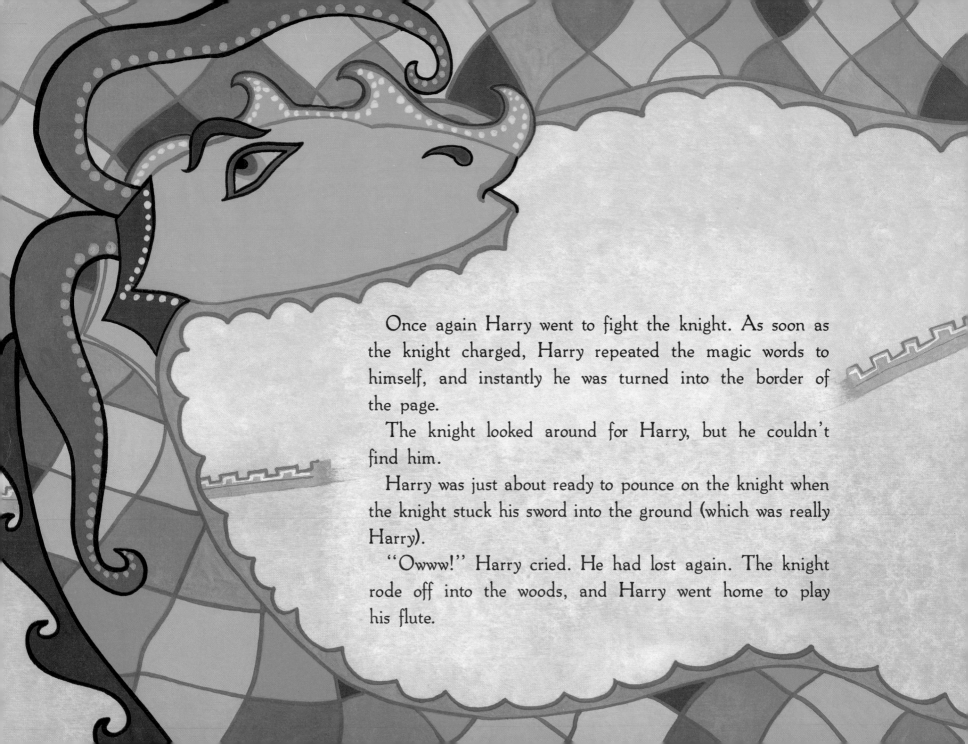

Once again Harry went to fight the knight. As soon as the knight charged, Harry repeated the magic words to himself, and instantly he was turned into the border of the page.

The knight looked around for Harry, but he couldn't find him.

Harry was just about ready to pounce on the knight when the knight stuck his sword into the ground (which was really Harry).

"Owww!" Harry cried. He had lost again. The knight rode off into the woods, and Harry went home to play his flute.

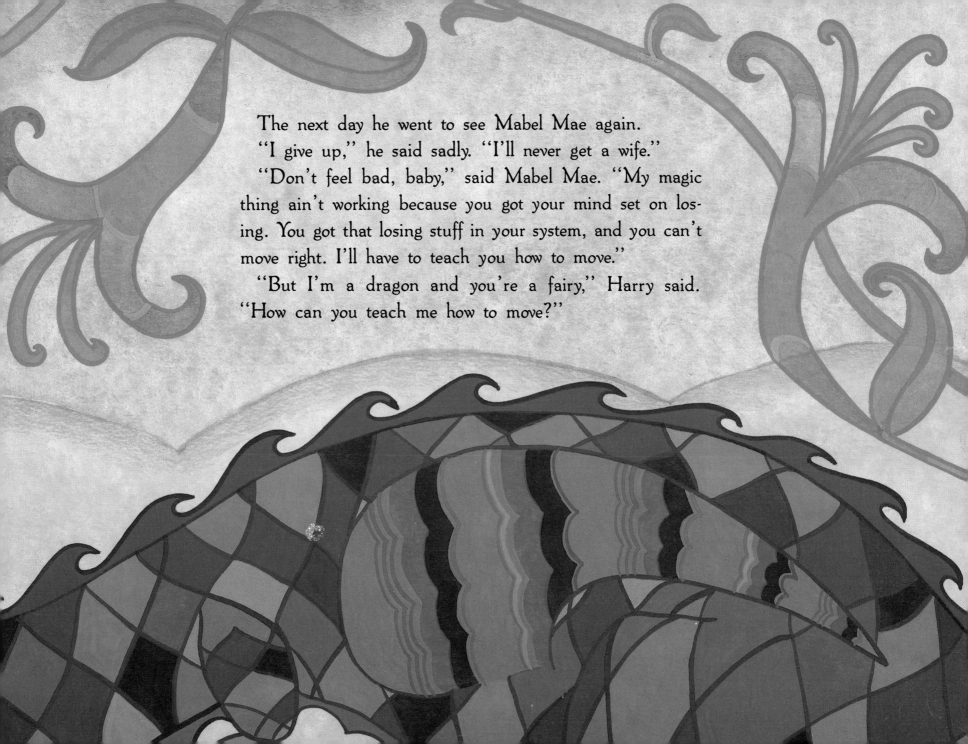

The next day he went to see Mabel Mae again.

"I give up," he said sadly. "I'll never get a wife."

"Don't feel bad, baby," said Mabel Mae. "My magic thing ain't working because you got your mind set on losing. You got that losing stuff in your system, and you can't move right. I'll have to teach you how to move."

"But I'm a dragon and you're a fairy," Harry said. "How can you teach me how to move?"

"That ain't no big thing," said Mabel Mae. Then she waved her wand and said the magic words.

Let me be a dragon
And teach Harry how to move
So that he can beat the knight
And get back in the groove."

And Mabel Mae turned into a dragon, the prettiest dragon Harry had ever seen.

"Watch me, Harry," she said. Then she started moving her shoulders up and down and swishing her tail from side to side.

But Harry could hardly keep his mind on her movements. She was so pretty!

"Gee, you're pretty, Mabel Mae," he said.

"You trying to get next to me, Harry?" asked Mabel Mae, blushing.

"If you remained a dragon," Harry said, "I could ask *you* to be my wife. Then I'd really have a reason for winning when I fought the knight."

"You know, I think we're into something, baby," Mabel Mae said. "I've always had a soft spot in my heart for dragons. Besides, I never did dig fairying too much."

So Harry went to the clearing to fight again. This time, when the knight charged, Harry moved his tail and shoulders the way Mabel Mae had shown him.

Then he whirled quickly around, flipped his tail at the knight, and knocked him down.

And that is the story of how Harry the dragon beat the knight, married Mabel Mae, got a good job in the post office, and lived happily ever after.

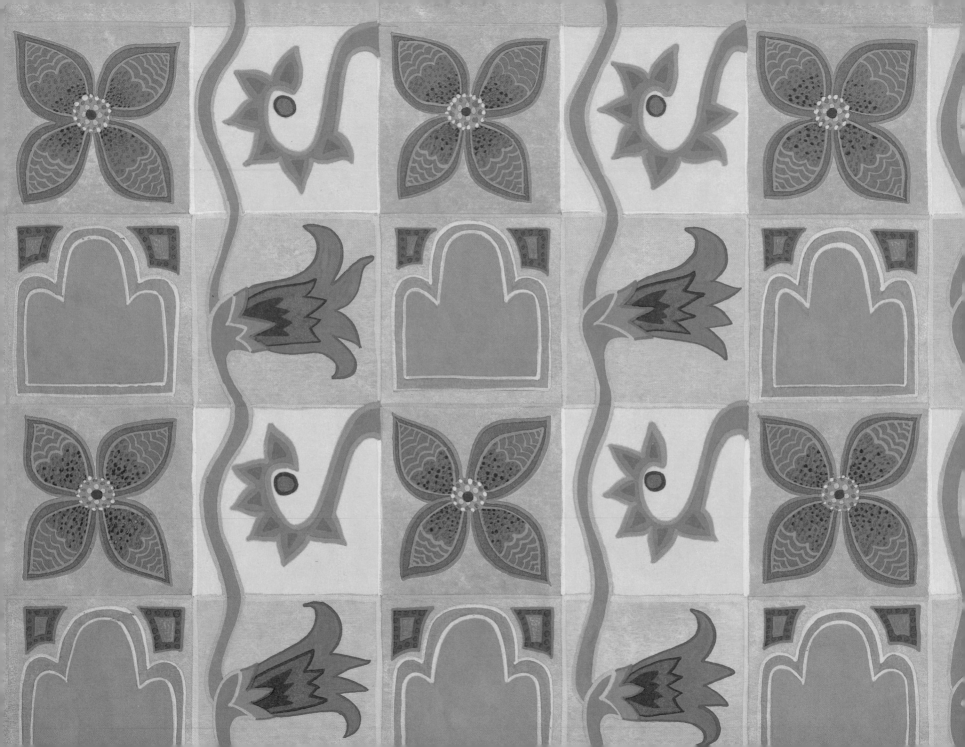